D0241971

This book belongs to

....

....

Where's Spot?

Eric Hill

PUFFIN

Sally
Spot

Naughty Spot!
It's dinner time.
Where can
he be?

Is he
behind
the door?

Is he inside the clock?

Is he
in the
piano?

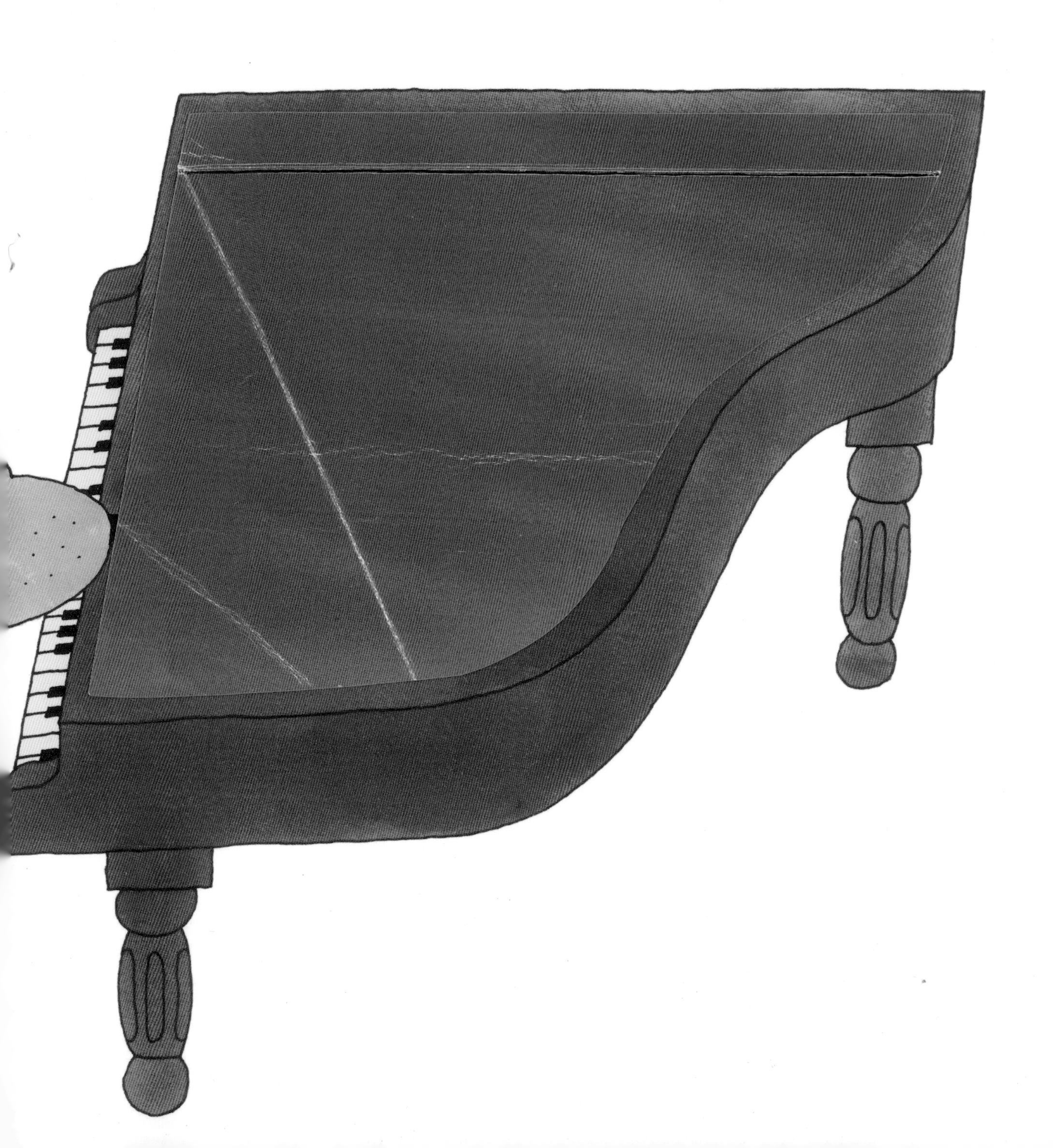

Is he under the stairs?

Is he in the wardrobe?

Is he
under the
bed?

Is he
in the
box?

There's Spot!

He's
under the
rug.

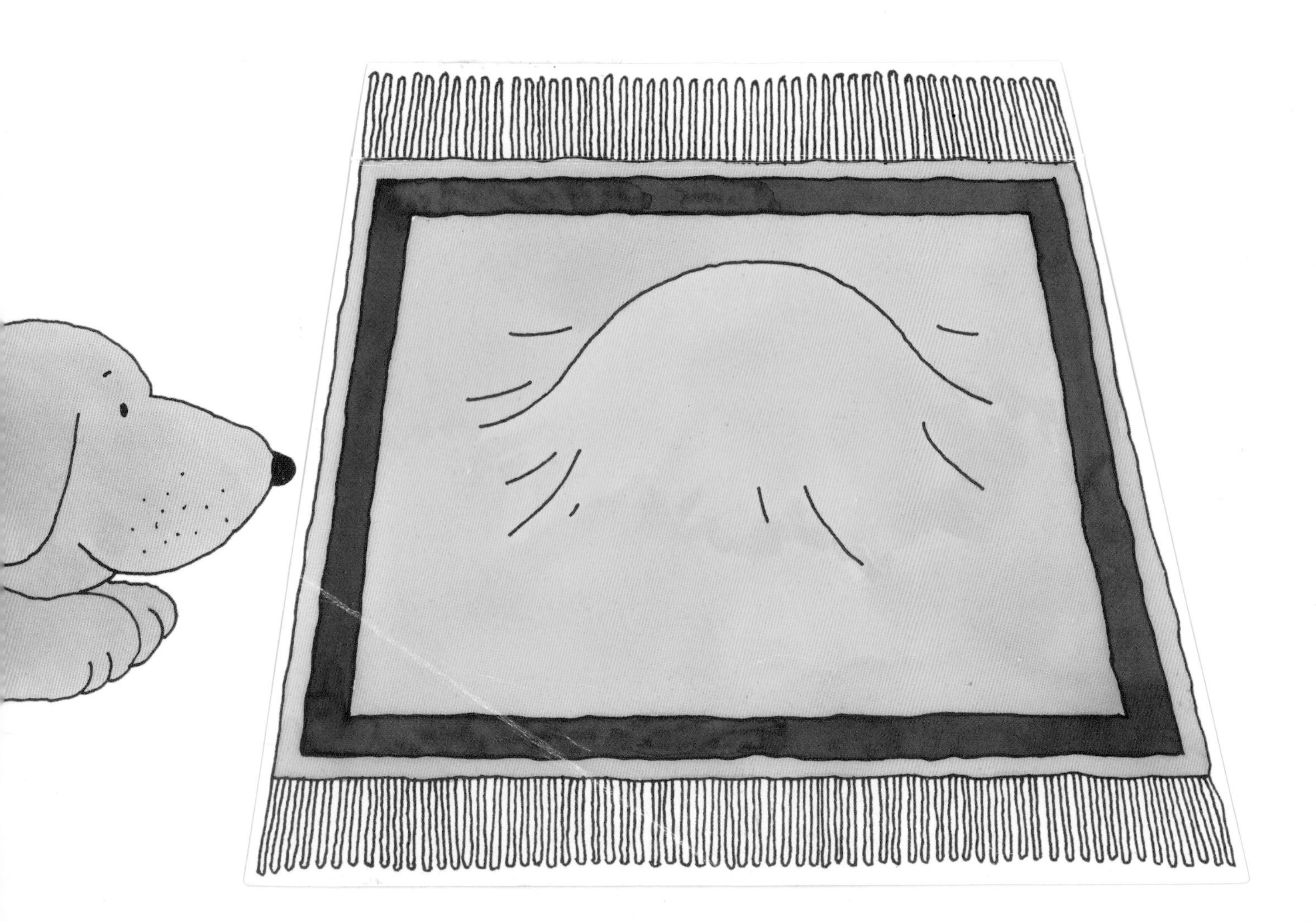

Sally

Good boy, Spot.
Eat up your
dinner!

PUFFIN BOOKS

UK | USA | Canada | Ireland | Australia | India | New Zealand | South Africa
Puffin Books is part of the Penguin Random House group of companies
whose addresses can be found at global.penguinrandomhouse.com.

www.penguin.co.uk www.puffin.co.uk www.ladybird.co.uk

First published by William Heinemann 1980
Published by Frederick Warne 1998
This edition published in Puffin Books 2020
001

Copyright © the Eric and Gillian Hill Family Trust, 1980
The moral right of the author/illustrator has been asserted

Printed in China

A CIP catalogue record for this book is available from the British Library

ISBN: 978–0–241–44685–0

Published by Penguin Random House Children's:
One Embassy Gardens, New Union Square,
5 Nine Elms Lane, London, SW8 5DA
Penguin Random House Australia Pty Ltd:
707 Collins Street, Melbourne, VIC 3008
Penguin Random House New Zealand:
67 Apollo Drive, Rosedale, Auckland 0632

Imported into the EEA by Penguin Random House Ireland,
Morrison Chambers, 32 Nassau Street, Dublin D02 YH68